The First G

'I saw your notice in
'I've come to order s
you get it for me I'll give you a sack full of golden
pieces. Ha, what do you say to that?'

'Jumping beetles!' cried Tuppeny, in delight.

'*Sounds* all right,' said Feefo.

'But what have we got to *get* for you?' asked
Jinks, cautiously.

'Oh, nothing much,' said the wizard, his cloak
flapping in Jinks's face as if a wind was blowing
it. 'I just want the Golden Bucket that belongs to
old Witch Grumble. She stole it from me a hundred years ago, and now I want it back.'

'Oh, yes, I've heard the story,' said Jinks. 'But
surely it isn't worth a whole sack of gold, Windy
Wizard?'

'Ah, but it's a magic bucket!' said the wizard,
his voice going down to a whisper.

Enid Blyton titles published by Red Fox

THE FIRST GREEN GOBLIN BOOK

by

Enid Blyton

Illustrated by
Paul Crompton

RED FOX

A Red Fox Book
Published by Random House Children's Books
20 Vauxhall Bridge Road, London SW1V 2SA

A division of The Random House Group Ltd
London Melbourne Sydney Auckland
Johannesburg and agencies throughout the world

First published as The Green Goblin Book by Newnes 1935
Shortened version (Feefo, Tuppeny and Jinks) published by Staples
Press 1951

Red Fox edition 1992

Set in Plantin
Typeset by JH Graphics Ltd, Reading

Printed and bound in Great Britain by
Cox & Wyman Ltd, Reading, Berkshire

THE RANDOM HOUSE GROUP
Limited Reg. no. 954009

ISBN 0 09 993700 X

Contents

Contents

How Feefo, Tuppeny and Jinks Met Together

Once upon a time, on a hot sunny afternoon, a little green goblin sat on a stile and wept loudly. He was a small, round fellow, dressed in a green tunic, tight yellow stockings, pointed green shoes and a pointed green hat with a yellow feather in it. His eyes were as green as the grass, and his nose was like a round button.

'Hoo-hoo!' he wept. 'It's terrible, terrible!'

Across the field behind him there came another goblin, dressed just the same. He was tall and thin, and his nose was long and crooked. His eyes shone as green as seawater. When he heard the first goblin howling he stopped in surprise.

'What's the matter?' he asked, poking the crying goblin in the back.

'Ooh! Don't!' said the little fat creature, wriggling. 'I'm ticklish, and you'll make me laugh.'

'Well, laugh then!' said the tall goblin, poking him again.

'I don't want to,' said the other. 'I want to cry. Hoo-hoo-hoo!'

'Why?' asked the tall goblin.

'Well,' said the little one, 'I've been turned out of my cave in the Green Hills, where I lived with my friends. They said I was lazy and wouldn't do my share of the work, the mean things!'

'*Didn't* you work?' asked the tall goblin.

'Yes, very hard,' said the other, 'but not like they did. They dug all day in the dark cold caves, looking for gold and for precious stones. I liked the sunshine, so I used to go and dig in a little garden I had, to make flowers grow, and to listen to the birds singing. I didn't want to be rich. But I didn't want to be turned out of my nice little cave with its flowery garden outside!'

'Cheer up,' said the tall goblin, and he waggled his pointed ears to and fro, which made the little goblin begin to laugh. 'Let's seek our fortune together. What is your name? Mine is Feefo.'

'Mine's Tuppeny,' said the little fat one, drying his eyes. 'Will you really be my friend and let me come with you? Where are you going?'

'I don't know,' said Feefo, scratching his long nose. 'I left my hill of goblins because they laughed at my long nose and pointed ears. I thought I would go out into the world and make my fortune somehow. Can you do anything clever, Tuppeny?'

'I can sing. Listen!' said Tuppeny, proudly. He opened his mouth, blew out his chest and began to sing a loud song at the top of his voice.

8

'Very nice,' said Feefo, hastily. 'That'll do. My ears aren't very strong today.'

'Can *you* do anything clever?' asked Tuppeny, when he had got his breath.

'Not *very* clever,' said Feefo, modestly. 'I can just make noises.'

'Noises! *What* noises?' asked Tuppeny, in surprise.

'Oh, any noises,' said Feefo. 'You know – a railway train – or a cackling goose – or the wind in the chimney at night.'

'Jumping beetles!' cried Tuppeny, in amazement. 'Let's hear you! Make a noise like a railway train whistling in a tunnel.'

'PheeeEEEEEEEEEEeeeeeeeeee!' whistled Feefo, at once, and Tuppeny was so startled that he looked round to see if a railway train was anywhere near. Feefo was pleased.

'Now I'll make a noise like a lion and a bear fighting together,' he said. He shut his eyes, opened his mouth, worked his throat about like a bird's, and made such a truly terrible noise that Tuppeny fell off the stile in alarm and hid under the nearest bush, trembling.

When Feefo opened his eyes Tuppeny was nowhere to be seen, and he was most surprised.

'Where are you?' he called. 'Don't go away.'

Tuppeny crawled from under the bush, and dusted his tunic.

'What were you doing there?' asked Feefo, in astonishment.

'Just looking for mushrooms,' said Tuppeny. 'Don't make any more noises just now, Feefo. Let's walk on together and talk about how we can make our fortune.'

They left the stile and walked over the field. They hadn't gone far before they saw a very strange creature coming towards them. They couldn't make it out at all. It had a large hat on, with a feather in it, but there didn't seem to be any face. The two goblins stopped in alarm.

'What is it?' said Tuppeny. 'I don't like it.'

'Nor do I,' said Feefo. 'Is it walking backwards, do you think? No, it can't be, because its boots are pointing this way. Ooh, what a strange creature!'

The creature came towards them, doing a little dance as it came. The hat wobbled on its head, and the goblins could *not* see any face however hard they looked.

When the creature was quite near it suddenly sprang upside down, landed on its 'head' and laughed loudly at the astonished faces of Feefo and Tuppeny.

'What's the matter?' asked the newcomer, grinning. 'Haven't you ever seen anyone walking on their hands before?'

'Oh – was *that* it?' said Feefo. 'But why did you put your hat on your feet? It made you look horrid, without any face, you know.'

'Well, if I put my hat on my head when I'm upside down, it falls off, silly!' grinned the goblin. 'Who are you? I'm Jinks.'

'This is Feefo and I'm Tuppeny,' said Tuppeny, who liked the look of the smiling goblin they had met. He was truly a strange-looking fellow, for his limbs seemed to be made of india-rubber, they were so long and supple. He had a cheerful,

11

smiling face with a very pointed chin, and his eyes, like theirs, were a bright, shining green.

Jinks took his boots off his hands and put them on his feet. Then he solemnly shook hands with Feefo and Tuppeny and said he was pleased to meet them.

'I'm a pedlar,' he said, showing them a small basket on his back, which opened unexpectedly into quite a large tray. On it were the most extraordinary things – a tin kettle, a white mouse that seemed quite at home on the tray, a roll of green ribbon, one yellow shoe, half a loaf of bread, a red toothbrush, and many other things. 'Do you want to buy anything?'

'No, thank you,' said Feefo, at once. 'We haven't any money. We are seeking our fortunes.'

'It's no good seeking fortunes,' said Jinks, shutting up his tray with a snap into a small basket again. 'There's none to be found. *I* know that, because haven't I been seeking a fortune all over the country for years? And have I ever found the tail-end of one? Never!'

'Well, where are fortunes to be found then?' asked Tuppeny, dismally.

'I'll tell you!' said Jinks, dancing along beside them. 'I've an idea, and it's a grand idea, too. There's never been such an idea before!'

'Tell us about it!' begged Tuppeny and Feefo, beginning to feel excited, and dancing along too.

'Well, listen to this,' said Jinks, stopping and

banging his fist on his hand. 'If you want bread you go to a baker's, don't you? And if you want meat, you go to a butcher's. But suppose you want the tail-feather of a cockyolly bird to wear in your hat. Where would you get that? Or a handkerchief that will tie itself into knots whenever you want to remember anything. Where would you go for that? Aha! That's where *I* come in!'

Tuppeny and Feefo were excited but puzzled. How did Jinks come in?

'Go on!' they cried, and Feefo's ears waggled in excitement.

'Well, *I'm* going to buy a little shop and supply anything marvellous, strange or impossible that people want, whether they are fairies, witches, goblins or elves!' cried Jinks, turning a complete somersault. 'What do you think of that for an idea? What about *that* for making my fortune? Why, suppose a witch wanted a tiggle-taggle spell for making twisty magic with – she'd give a whole bag of gold to get it, wouldn't she! Then think how rich I'd be!'

'But – but – do you think you could get all these strange things that people might want?' asked Feefo, doubtfully.

'Ah, you don't know me!' said Jinks. 'I'm a clever chap, I am. All I want is a couple of friends to help me. What about you two?'

'Yes, we will!' said Feefo and Tuppeny at once, feeling pleased to think that a clever fellow like

13

Jinks should ask them. So off they all went together, talking nineteen to the dozen. Jinks sometimes walked on his hands and sometimes on his feet, and once or twice he joined his arms and legs together and rolled down a hill like a ball. You never knew what he was going to do next.

He was very pleased when he found that Feefo could make such extraordinary noises. He made him croak like a frog, cluck like three hens, snore like a hedgehog and rattle like twenty dustbin lids. It was really marvellous to hear Feefo. Then Tuppeny wanted to sing, but Jinks said he didn't like singing, and every time poor Tuppeny started he tickled him so that he laughed too much to go on.

That night they slept under a hedge, and cooked for breakfast some eggs and bacon that Jinks had with him. They then walked on over the fields and at last came to a pretty little village called Heyho.

And it was there that Jinks saw the very cottage he wanted for his fine new shop!

You should have seen it! It was a dear little place with a thatched roof, a curly chimney and a garden full of hollyhocks and sweet-williams, pansies and white daisies, lavender and stocks. It smelt sweet, it looked sweet and it *was* sweet!

'This shall be our cottage!' said Jinks, standing by the gate. 'We'll move in at once.'

On the gate was the name – Hollyhock Cottage. There was a big oblong window, made of small diamond-shaped panes, along the front of the cottage and Jinks said that they could put their goods there for everyone to see.

Well, they moved in. They bought three tiny beds, three small chairs and a little round table. Jinks took a kettle from his basket, a saucepan and a teapot. It was really a marvellous basket he had – it seemed to be full of different things each time, though the little white mouse was always there.

The three goblins were soon very busy. They

painted the cottage white all over. They made a sign-board and on it they painted 'The Green Goblins'. They put some strange things in the

window, out of Jink's basket, and then Feefo printed a big notice to put in the window too. This is what he put –

WE SUPPPLY ANYTHING IN THE
WORLD FOR WITCHES, FAIRIES,
ELVES OR NOMES

Jinks said that 'supply' should only have one P,

and Tuppeny said it should have two. So Feefo put in one P for Jinks and two for Tuppeny to stop them quarrelling. Nobody knew that 'Nomes' was spelt wrong. It looked quite all right to them.

Then they waited for customers. They peeped behind the curtains in excitement and watched all the people come and read the notice in the window.

Three fairies came. Then a pixie ran up with tiny wings on her feet. Then an old witch hobbled up, using her magic broomstick as a walking stick. Then two gnomes with long beards reaching down to the ground.

They all read the notice, nodded their heads at one another, chattered about the new shop and went away. Nobody came in at all. It was most disappointing.

'I don't think much of your idea for making fortunes, Jinks,' said Tuppeny, gloomily, as he put the kettle on to make a cup of cocoa for supper.

Feefo made a noise like a hippopotamus with toothache and made Tuppeny jump so much that he dropped the kettle on to Jinks's toe. Jinks at once made a noise like Jinks being very angry and rushed at Tuppeny, who dodged behind the sofa in the corner.

'Oh! Ah! Ooh!' yelled Tuppeny, as Jinks pulled him out by the legs.

And then – and then – just as there was a

perfectly terrible noise going on, a big, deep voice came down the chimney and startled the three goblins almost out of their wits.

'HOO!' said the voice. 'HOO-HOO! I'm coming down the chimney! I'm the Windy Wizard and I'm sitting up on the roof. I want to come and buy something.'

'Don't come down the chimney!' called Jinks in a fright. 'There's a fire in the grate and you'll burn your toes. Come to the door.'

The Golden
Witch-bucket

But the Windy Wizard took no notice of Jinks. He came down the chimney! First of all a great draught blew down into the grate, and ashes went flying all over the kitchen. The fire went out with a strange pop and sizzle. Then two skinny bare feet appeared down the chimney.

'Hi! Give me a tug!' called the Windy Wizard. 'Your chimney's small and I'm stuck.'

Jinks rushed forward and caught hold of the wizard's legs. He pulled and the wizard came down with a rush. He sat in the fireplace and blinked at the three goblins. He was a very strange fellow indeed.

He wore a gold suit that fitted him like a skin, and over it a long cloak that flowed down to the ground and was never still. It was black, set with little twinkling stars. On his head was a tall, pointed hat that kept slipping over one eye because it was just a little too big. He wore a pair of large green spectacles on his long nose.

'Don't you think you'd better get out of the

fireplace?' asked Feefo, anxiously. 'You blew the fire out, but I expect the coal is still hot.'

'It does feel a bit warm,' said the Windy Wizard, and he got up and came into the room.

'Ooh! Jumping beetles! You've burnt a big hole in your lovely cloak!' cried little Tuppeny, and he pointed to a large hole in the wizard's long cloak.

The wizard licked his thumb and passed it over the burn. In a trice the hole had disappeared and the cloak was as good as new.

'Won't you sit down?' asked Feefo, who was always the polite one. He pulled a chair out and the wizard sat down, his strange cloak swirling out round him. The three goblins shivered, for there seemed to be a wind in the room, and a very cold one it was for summertime.

'I saw your notice in the window,' said the wizard. 'I've come to order something from you – and if you get it for me I'll give you a sack full of golden pieces. Ha, what do you say to that?'

'Jumping beetles!' cried Tuppeny, in delight.

'*Sounds* all right,' said Feefo.

'But what have we got to *get* for you?' asked Jinks, cautiously.

'Oh, nothing much,' said the wizard, his cloak flapping in Jinks's face as if a wind was blowing it. 'I just want the Golden Bucket that belongs to old Witch Grumble. She stole it from me a hundred years ago, and now I want it back.'

'Oh, yes, I've heard the story,' said Jinks. 'But surely it isn't worth a whole sack of gold, Windy Wizard?'

'Ah, but it's a magic bucket!' said the wizard, his voice going down to a whisper. 'You know, whatever you throw into it disappears at once – such a useful way to get rid of rubbish. You've no idea what a lot of rubbish I have when I'm making spells, and there's no dustman where I live. My whole garden is piled with rubbish and I'm tired of it. If I could get my bucket back I could live tidily and pleasantly, for I could just throw anything I didn't want into the bucket and it would be gone for ever!'

'But where does the Grumble Witch live?' asked Feefo.

'She lives on a hill in the middle of the Dancing Sea,' said the wizard. 'And pray be careful of her, for she has a very nasty temper. I should be sorry to hear you had been turned into beetles, because you look nice little fellows.'

'J-j-j-jumping b-b-b-beetles!' said Tuppeny, in a fright.

'No, not jumping beetles, just ordinary beetles,' said the wizard. 'Well, I must go. Let me know when you have the Golden Witch-bucket, and I'll bring you your reward.'

He stood up and a draught whistled through the room again, making the goblins feel very cold. The black cloak wrapped itself tightly round the wizard, the candle went out, and when the goblins had lighted it again the Windy Wizard was gone! Goodness knows where he went to!

'Our first order!' said Jinks, rubbing his long hands together, pleased. 'We'll start off tomorrow.'

'I don't w-w-w-want to,' said poor Tuppeny, beginning to cry. He felt frightened.

'Don't be silly,' said Jinks, putting his arm round the fat little goblin. '*We*'ll look after you, Tuppeny. Cheer up! We are going to make our fortunes!'

22

They went to bed at once and blew out the candle. They awoke early, full of excitement. They shut up the shop, first putting a notice in the window, which said –

> **GONE ON BIZNESS**
> **FOR OUR ONNERED**
> **CUSTUMER THE WINDY**
> **WIZZARD**

Then Jinks slipped his pedlar's basket round his neck, in which he had put their toothbrushes, towels, a piece of soap, and some clean pairs of stockings. The little white mouse was excited to see the soap, and Tuppeny was afraid it might eat it. But Jinks said it wouldn't.

Then they slammed the door of Hollyhock Cottage and set off together, Tuppeny singing a very loud song indeed, and Feefo making a noise like a motorcar gone wrong. Jinks turned head-over-heels a few times, so it was no wonder that Heyho Village looked out of their windows in wonder at the three happy goblins.

'How do we get to the Dancing Sea?' asked Tuppeny

'I've looked it up on a map,' said Jinks. 'If we take the bus to Breezy Corner, we can get a boat

there on the Rushing River. It goes down to the
Dancing Sea. We are sure to be able to see the
Witch's Hill then.'

'How shall we get the bucket from her?' asked
Tuppeny.

'Oh, we don't need to think of that till we get
there!' said Jinks, impatiently.

The bus was coming down the lane and the
goblins hopped on to it. It was crowded with
rabbits going to the Lettuce and Carrot Market in
the next village. They were very hot to sit next to
on a warm summer's day. Fat little Tuppeny
began to puff and blow, and the rabbits next to
him looked at him crossly.

'Will you please stop blowing my whiskers
about?' said one, sternly. 'If you don't, I shall
complain to the conductor.'

Tuppeny made himself as small as possible,
blushed very red, and tried not to puff and blow.
Jinks laughed loudly, and Feefo began to make a
noise like seven dogs growling, barking and yelp-
ing. With one accord the rabbits rose up and fled
from the bus.

'Where are those dogs?' asked the conductor,
peering into the bus. 'If you've brought dogs with
you, you must buy dog-tickets. Anyway, you
ought to know better than to bring dogs into a bus
where there are rabbit passengers.'

The three goblins looked innocent, and Jinks
got up and looked under the seat for the dogs that

he knew weren't there. That made Tuppeny giggle, and the conductor looked sternly at the goblins and said they had better behave themselves or he wouldn't have them in his bus.

After that they sat quietly, and very soon they came to Breezy Corner. The conductor didn't need to call out the name, for it was so windy that the bus nearly blew over! The three goblins tumbled out and looked for the Rushing River.

'There it is, over there!' cried Tuppeny, and they all set off as fast as they could go. There were many little boats tethered to the bank, but none had any oars.

'You don't need oars on this river,' said the pixie in charge of them. 'The river runs so fast that it takes you along without oars. You can't go *up* the river because the current is too strong.'

'But how do the boats come back to you?' asked Jinks, in astonishment.

'Oh, I keep a flock of swans and they bring all my boats back once a day,' said the pixie. He pointed to a swan swimming strongly up the Rushing River. It pulled a little boat behind it quite easily.

The goblins got into a boat and the pixie set it loose. It bounced off into the current and the three goblins held on tightly! Jinks guided the boat as best he could and shouted to Tuppeny not to lean over the side, or he might fall in. Tuppeny took no notice and Feefo just grabbed him in time to save him from falling head-over-heels in the water. The boat rocked dangerously and everyone got splashed.

'You silly, stupid goblin!' shouted Jinks, in a temper. 'I've a good mind to leave you behind if you don't do as you're told!'

Tuppeny opened his mouth and howled in despair at being talked to like that. So Feefo put his arm round him and comforted him, though Jinks frowned for about five minutes and nearly

guided them into the bank. Then they all forgot their troubles and began to look for the Dancing Sea.

The river became wider and wider, and at last flowed into a bright blue sea. It was a strange sea, for, although there were no waves that broke, little dancing ripples and lines of white foam jigged up and down all the time. The boat jigged too, and Feefo turned green. He didn't like it at all!

'I shall be seasick!' he groaned.

'Oh, no, you won't!' said Jinks, at once, and he opened his wonderful basket. It spread out like a tray and Tuppeny saw the white mouse nibbling at their soap.

'There! I told you that mouse would eat our soap!' he cried. 'I shall put it into my pocket!'

He took the soap away and slipped it into his green tunic pocket. The mouse squeaked at him angrily and ran inside a green shoe that was on the tray. Jinks picked up a little green packet and shook out a pill, which he gave to poor, green-faced Feefo.

'Swallow that, and you'll be all right.' he said.

Feefo swallowed it, and then, to everyone's surprise and alarm, he immediately began to grow twice as large as he had been, and the boat rocked dangerously.

'Ooh! I've given him the wrong pill!' said Jinks, in fright. 'Quick, Feefo, swallow this one instead!'

Poor Feefo swallowed it, and to Jinks's and Tuppeny's relief he went back to his own size again.

'Now I feel more seasick than ever,' said the poor goblin, holding his head in his hand. His long, pointed ears drooped down like a rabbit's, and Tuppeny felt very sorry for him.

Jinks scrabbled about on his tray and at last found some more green pills. He gave one to Feefo, and as it really was the right one this time Feefo soon cheered up and felt better.

Then Jinks took a look round to see where they were. Dear me, they were quite out of sight of land! The blue sea lay all round them, dancing up and down in the sunshine, jigging into little points, rippling gaily.

'Where are we?' cried Tuppeny, in alarm.

'Where do you suppose?' said Jinks. 'Sitting on someone's chimney-top?'

Feefo giggled, but Tuppeny frowned. He didn't like being laughed at. He looked all round him and then he suddenly gave a loud shout.

'See! There's the Witch's Hill!'

The others looked. Sure enough, far away on the horizon, a steep hill rose up out of the sea. It looked rather small to the three goblins because they were far away, but as they drew nearer they saw that it was really a very big hill indeed.

At last the boat grated on the shingly beach of the island hill. The three goblins jumped out and looked at the castle that stood high up on the top. A long, long flight of steps led up to it.

'Ooh dear!' said fat little Tuppeny, when he

saw all those steps. 'I shall never get up to the top!'

'Well, you've got to!' said Jinks. 'Because *you're* going to get the Golden Witch-bucket!'

'*Me!*' cried Tuppeny, in alarm. 'Oh, I couldn't!'

'Now, just listen to my plan,' said Jinks, and they all sat down on the beach. 'It's perfectly simple. In fact, it's a plan that's been used before very successfully. Do you remember in the story of Aladdin how the magician there got back the magic lamp?'

'Yes, he went round shouting "New Lamps for Old!" ' said Feefo, at once. 'And he got the old magic lamp back in return for a new one that wasn't magic.'

'Yes,' said Jinks. 'Well, that's what I thought

29

we'd do. I'll get a nice new pail out of my basket
and Tuppeny shall take it up to the castle and
offer it to the servants there in return for any old
one they have. Then perhaps they'll give him the
Witch-bucket!'

'And perhaps they won't!' said Feefo.

'I'm not going to go up to the castle alone,' said
Tuppeny, firmly. 'If your plan is so good, Jinks,
you'd better do it yourself. I shall only make a
muddle of it.'

'No, I chose you because you look such a nice,
fat, jolly little fellow,' said Jinks. 'Nobody would
ever think you would play a clever trick on them.
Go on, Tuppeny, just try. We will come up the
steps with you, and we'll hide somewhere and
watch what happens. You won't be alone.'

'All right,' said Tuppeny. 'But if anything
happens to me, promise me something, both of
you – save me somehow, won't you?'

'Of course,' said Jinks and Feefo together, and
they hugged the fat, solemn little goblin.

Then they began to climb up the steps to the
witch's castle. Oh, what a long way! How they
panted and puffed, how they sighed and
grumbled!

At last they reached the top. In front of them
was the castle yard, and the back door stood wide
open. A great noise of chattering came out from
it, and clouds of steam rushed out of the door.

'Washing day!' whispered Jinks to the others.

'That means there will be lots of pails used and perhaps the servants will be pleased to have a new one from Tuppeny, in exchange for the old Witch-bucket. It must be very old and dirty now.'

Jinks opened his basket and made it into a tray. In the very middle stood a marvellous, shining, new bucket!

'Jumping beetles!' said Tuppeny, in surprise. 'Look at that!'

'Look at that!'

Jinks gave the bucket to Tuppeny and pushed him towards the kitchen door of the castle. 'Go on!' he said. 'Do your best.'

Rather shaky at the knees, poor little Tuppeny marched over to the kitchen door. The others heard him shout in his high voice.

'New buckets for old! New buckets for old!'

A fat and untidy cook came to the door. She looked kindly at little Tuppeny and smiled at him.

'Well, my little man,' she said. 'So you've come to our castle, have you? What's that you've got? A fine new bucket?'

'Yes, and you can have it for an old one,' said Tuppeny.

'That's funny!' said the cook, looking hard at Tuppeny. He felt uncomfortable. Perhaps it did sound strange to offer a new bucket for an old one.

'Well, you can give me a good meal too, if

you like,' he said, smiling up at the kindly faced cook.

'Ah, I thought you'd want something else, too!' she said, patting him on the shoulder. 'Well, wait a minute, mannikin, and you shall have a fine dinner. I'll set you a little table in the yard here, for the scullery and kitchen are full of steam. I can do with a new bucket today. My old one has a leak in it.'

She took the shining new bucket from Tuppeny, and gave him an old, rusty one, with a hole in the bottom. Jinks and Feefo, who were watching from behind a tree, were simply delighted to see how easily their plan had worked. They expected Tuppeny to come rushing over to them – but he didn't.

Instead he sat himself down at a little table the cook brought out and then, to the other goblins' envy and disgust, the fat little fellow set to work to eat a lovely dinner that the cook set before him.

She gave him four fried sausages, a large potato, six fried tomatoes and a great deal of gravy. For his pudding he had a piece of suet with a great lake of golden treacle round it.

Jinks and Feefo, who had had nothing to eat since they left home, were very jealous. They sniffed the good dinner, and each of them wished he had gone to the kitchen door instead of Tuppeny. That little goblin turned round and beamed in triumph at them. The old bucket stood beside him, and Jinks longed to get hold of it. Suppose anything happened to it before Tuppeny came to them? Suppose the old witch came out and saw it?

But nothing at all happened to the old bucket. It just stood there whilst Tuppeny ate his dinner.

Poor Little Tuppeny

When Tuppeny had finished his dinner he took his plates to a pump in the yard and carefully washed them. Then he went to the kitchen door and called to the cook. The servants were having their dinner and at first they did not hear Tuppeny's voice. So he walked into the scullery and looked round.

The the cook saw him and hustled him out. 'No one's allowed to come inside!' she cried. 'Shoo, little mannikin, shoo!'

Tuppeny was frightened. He gave the cook the plates and fled, taking the rusty old bucket with him. As soon as he reached Feefo and Jinks they took the bucket from him in delight.

'You were lucky to get a good meal like that,' said Jinks, enviously.

'Well, I earned it!' said Tuppeny. 'Wasn't I clever and brave enough to go and get the Witch-bucket for you? I deserved a good meal.'

'Let's throw some rubbish into the bucket and see it disappear,' said Jinks, who was longing to

try the Witch-bucket's strange powers. So Feefo
picked up a paper bag that was blowing round the
yard and some twigs from under a tree. He threw
them all into the bucket and the three goblins
bent over it excitedly to see them vanish out of
sight.

But they didn't! No, they just stayed in the
bucket and didn't go away at all. Jinks put in his
hand and stirred the rubbish round a bit. No good
at all! It just stayed there all the same.

'Jumping beetles!' said Tuppeny. 'It can't be
the right bucket!'

The three sat down and looked at one another
in dismay. What a terrible shock!

Then Tuppeny had an idea and he jumped to
his feet in excitement.

'Of course! I *saw* the right bucket when I went
into the scullery just now! It must be the one. It
was hanging on a nail over the sink, and it was
shining like gold. Why should we think the
Witch-bucket ought to be old and dirty? It is
much more likely to be well polished and shining
bright!'

'Ooh!' said Jinks and Feefo at once, their faces
brightening. 'Ooh! Then, Tuppeny, you could
perhaps just go across and get the bucket?'

'Why shouldn't *you*?' demanded Tuppeny,
fiercely. 'I've had my turn.'

'Yes – but you know where the bucket is and
we don't,' said Jinks at once.

'All right, all right,' said Tuppeny, sighing. 'I'll go – but if I get caught, remember what you promised, you two. You said you would rescue me.'

'Of course,' said Jinks and Feefo, together. 'Go on, now, Tuppeny, whilst the servants are having dinner in the kitchen.'

So Tuppeny crept softly across the yard again and peeped in at the scullery. No servants were there. It was quite empty. He tiptoed inside, went to the sink and unhooked the shining bucket from its nail. Then he turned to run.

But poor little Tuppeny tripped over a mat and down he went, the bucket clanging behind him on the floor! Oh dear!

A loud and angry voice came from the kitchen and someone ran to the scullery. It was the Grumble Witch herself, followed by all the surprised servants. Tuppeny gave a screech when he saw the green-eyed witch and ran for his life, taking the bucket with him.

The witch ran after him, shouting and roaring in rage.

'Bring me back my bucket, you wicked little goblin!'

'It isn't yours, it belongs to the Windy Wizard!' yelled Tuppeny.

Jinks and Feefo, when they saw the old witch pounding along, her bright red dress flying out behind her, were full of alarm. They rushed to the

castle steps and ran down them as quickly as ever they could. They were soon at the bottom and they looked up, hoping that Tuppeny would join them, then they could run and hide.

Tuppeny was tearing down the steep steps as fast as his fat little legs could carry him. Suddenly he slipped and dropped the bucket, which went clanging and bumping down the steps to the very bottom, where it stood upright. Tuppeny rolled over and over too, and at last reached the bottom – but oh my goodness gracious, what *do* you suppose happened? Why, Tuppeny fell straight into the big Witch-bucket – and, of course, as it really *was* the magic bucket this time, he disappeared!

Jinks, thinking that Tuppeny was inside the bucket, caught it up and ran off with it, Feefo beside him. They ran to the boat they had left on the beach, and, what a pleasant surprise! A big white swan was there, too, waiting to take the boat back to the pixie on the Rushing River!

The two goblins tumbled into the boat and the swan at once swam off quickly. The witch stood on the shore and shook her fist at them. Then she suddenly cried out a strange magic spell, and to the goblins' great alarm, the sea began to heave up enormous waves and toss the little boat about like a cork.

'This isn't a *Dancing* Sea, this is a Jumping and Skipping Sea!' groaned poor Feefo, who was feeling very seasick again. 'I say, Jinks, we shall be wrecked!'

But the swan saved them. It didn't like the choppy sea, so it suddenly spread its great white wings and flew up into the air, taking the boat with it on a rope!

Jinks and Feefo nearly fell out! Jinks clutched the side of the boat and the bucket just in time. Feefo clung on with both hands and stopped feeling seasick. The witch could do nothing more, and they saw her climbing up the steep steps to her castle.

'Get Tuppeny out of the bucket,' said Feefo to Jinks. 'He'll be more comfortable in the boat.'

Jinks looked into the big bucket and spoke.

'Hallo, there, Tuppeny, come out! You're safe now.'

But, of course, there was no Tuppeny there! The bucket was empty. Jinks gave a scream and turned pale.

'What's the matter?' asked Feefo, scared.

'Tuppeny's gone!' said Jinks, tears coming into his eyes.

'*Gone!* What do you mean, *gone*?' said Feefo.

'Just gone,' said Jinks, wiping his eyes. 'Oh, Feefo, don't you see what has happened? This is the magic bucket, and when Tuppeny tumbled into it he went the way of any rubbish that is put in. He disappeared!'

Feefo was so horrified that his hair stood straight up from his head and his hat fell off into the boat. He couldn't say a word. But tears poured down his thin cheeks, for he was very fond of little fat Tuppeny.

'W-w-w-w-what shall we d-d-d-do?' sniffed Jinks. 'How can we get T-t-t-tuppeny back?'

'We promised to save him if anything ever happened to him,' said Feefo, finding his voice at last.

'Perhaps the Windy Wizard can tell us how to save him,' said Jinks, drying his eyes. 'Do you mind turning the other way if you want to cry any more, Feefo? Your tears are making a puddle round my feet.'

'Sorry,' said Feefo, feeling about for his handkerchief. 'Oh, Jinks, this is terrible. Poor little Tuppeny! To think we made him get the bucket for us! It's all our fault!'

'Well, we'll ask the Windy Wizard to help us,' said Jinks. 'He's sure to know where Tuppeny has gone. Then when we know we'll go and rescue him.

The swan flew on and on over the stormy sea. When it reached the Rushing River it flew down to the water again and the boat flopped on to the river. Then very swiftly the swan swam up the river until it reached the place where the little pixie kept his boats.

Jinks and Feefo jumped out, paid the pixie and hurried off to catch the bus back to Heyho Village. It was full of rabbits again, this time going back from the Lettuce and Carrot Market, but the two goblins felt so sad that they played no tricks at all. They sat quietly in a corner, sometimes sniffing sadly when they thought of poor little Tuppeny.

They got out at Hollyhock Cottage and went sorrowfully up the path. Then Jinks wrote a letter to the Windy Wizard and told him he had got the magic Witch-bucket and please would he call and fetch it.

That night the wizard came. Once more he came down the chimney and blew the fire out. He looked all round the kitchen very eagerly for his bucket, but he couldn't see it. In his hand he carried a small sack which chinked when he put it down. But even the sound of so many gold pieces couldn't make Jinks and Feefo smile.

'Great elephants! What's the matter with you?' asked the wizard in amazement. 'Are you bewitched?'

'No, but poor Tuppeny is!' said Jinks; and he told the Windy Wizard all that had happened.

'Well, I can't help that,' said the wizard,

impatiently. 'That bucket is all I care about. It's your own carelessness that lost you your companion. Give me the bucket and take your pay.'

'We want you to tell us where Tuppeny is,' said Jinks, firmly. 'We've got to rescue him.'

'I can't waste my time chattering to you,' said the wizard, his black, twinkling cloak swirling out round him as if it were impatient. 'Give me my bucket and let me go.'

'No, you shan't have the bucket until you tell us where Tuppeny is,' said Feefo and Jinks both together.

'Well, he's gone where all the rubbish goes,' said the wizard.

'Where's that?' asked Jinks, in dismay.

'In the great caves of the Hoo-Moo-Loos,' said the wizard, wrapping his cloak tightly round him. 'You'll have to go to the end of the rainbow, find a toadstool with six red spots underneath and let it take you down to the caves. The King is an odd chap called Tick-Tock because he loves to have hundreds of clocks all round him. He may want to keep you prisoner if you go there, so be careful. Now where's that bucket?'

Jinks took it from a cupboard and placed it in front of the delighted wizard. He danced round it and clapped his hands for joy. It stood there, big and shining, made of pure gold.

'Give me some paper and let me see if the magic is still in it,' said the wizard.

42

'Well, of course it's still magic,' cried Jinks, impatiently. 'How do you suppose Tuppeny disappeared if the bucket isn't magic?'

But the wizard wanted to make certain. So Feefo and Jinks took an old newspaper and crammed it into the bucket. It vanished at once! Then they emptied the tea leaves out of their teapot. Those disappeared too. Then Jinks, in a moment of mischief, seized the end of the wizard's long cloak and stuffed that into the bucket as well. The wizard gave a yell and tugged it out again at once, before it had had time to disappear.

'Stupid, silly creature!' he cried, and gave Jinks a box on the ear. 'I've a good mind to put *you* in!'

'Sorry,' said Jinks, half-frightened. 'Take your bucket, wizard, and leave us the gold.'

The wizard picked up the bucket, blew out the candle on the table and disappeared in a swirl of black cloak. Jinks and Feefo couldn't make out if he had gone through the door, jumped out of the window or flown up the chimney. He was really a very strange visitor.

The two goblins undid the sack. It was full of shining gold pieces!

'There's a fortune for you!' cried Jinks. But Feefo shook his head sadly.

'What's the good of a fortune if you lose a good friend? Put the gold away in a cupboard, Jinks, and let us think of Tuppeny instead. The very

next time we see a rainbow we must set off to find the end of it.'

So the gold was put away, and the two sad little goblins undressed themselves and got into bed, after having a cup of very hot cocoa and two pieces of brown bread and butter each.

'Good night, Jinks,' said Feefo.

'Good night, Feefo,' said Jinks. 'I do wonder what poor little Tuppeny is doing, don't you?'

The Land of the Hoo-Moo-Loos

The next day was fine with never a spot of rain. The day after was fine, too, but in the morning a raincloud blew up and a shower fell. At the same time the sun shone and a lovely rainbow glowed from the clouds to the earth.

'Look! Quick!' cried Jinks, and ran out into the garden. 'See, Feefo! The end of the rainbow is touching the Tiptop Hill over there. Can you see?'

'Yes,' said Feefo, screwing up his eyes. 'It is just touching that gorse-bush, I think. Come on, Jinks, put on your basket and your hat and we'll go. There might not be another rainbow for weeks, and we must rescue Tuppeny as soon as ever we can. He will be very unhappy all by himself in a strange country.'

Off they went across the fields towards Tiptop Hill. This was a fairly steep hill, covered with gorse and bracken. The goblins toiled up it to the gorse-bush that they had thought was touched by the end of the rainbow. The rainbow had long since vanished, of course, but the gorse-bush was still there.

They came to it at last. 'Now we must hunt for a toadstool with six red spots underneath,' said Feefo. So they searched all round and about. But there was no toadstool at all.

'Perhaps it's under the gorse-bush,' said Jinks, at last.

'Ooh! I hope not!' said Feefo. 'It's so prickly!'

But that's just where it was! Jinks crawled right underneath and gave a shout.

'It's here – quite a large one. My, it's prickly under this bush. Be careful, Feefo, or you'll be scratched to bits!'

Feefo crawled under, groaning. He saw the toadstool at once and looked underneath it. Sure enough, it had six red spots.

'I suppose we sit on it and wish to be taken to the Land of the Hoo-Moo-Loos,' said Jinks. There was hardly room to squeeze himself on to the toadstool, but he and Feefo managed somehow. Then Jinks wished.

WhhhhoooooooOOOOOOOOOOOOOSH!

What a surprise for the goblins! The toadstool sank downwards at a terrific speed, taking their breath away! They clung tightly to it, afraid of tumbling off. They couldn't possibly see what they were passing for the toadstool went far too quickly.

'It's a sort of lift,' shouted Jinks to Feefo. The

toadstool was making such a loud whooshing noise that he had to shout.

Ker-plunk! The toadstool came to a sudden stop and the goblins bounced off at once.

'Ooh!' said Jinks, rubbing his bruised leg.

'Ow!' groaned Feefo, feeling his arms to see if they were broken.

'Tickets, please,' said a booming voice and a very large mole, dressed like a ticket-collector, came out of the darkness towards them. They were far underground and the cave they were in was lighted by one green lamp swinging from the roof.

'Tickets!' said Jinks, indignantly. 'What do you mean, tickets! We haven't any!'

'You ought to have tickets if you use our lift,' said the mole severely, waving his spade-like paws about. 'Everybody does. You'd better come with me.'

Now Jinks certainly didn't want to be marched off and locked up anywhere so he racked his brains to think what to do. Then a bright idea came to him.

'Feefo!' he whispered. 'If there's one thing that moles like more than another, it's worms. Can you make a noise like a dozen worms having a tea-party, do you think?'

'Easy!' said Feefo, and at once a most curious sound filled the cave. It made you think of wrigglings, squirmings and writhings, and the mole at once began to twitch his sensitive nose.

'Worms!' he muttered. 'Where are they? A whole lot of them by the sound! But I can't smell them! Ooh, worms, worms!'

He rushed off into a corner and began to dig violently, forgetting all about Jinks and Feefo, who were giggling softly together. 'Come on,' whispered Feefo. 'He's safe for a few minutes!'

So they stole off into another cave, hearing an excited mutter behind them in the dark corner of the cave, of 'Worms, wor-r-rums, worms!'

The two goblins went through cave after cave. Some were dark, some were lighter. Some were enormous, some were very small, so small that Feefo and Jinks had to duck their heads when walking through them.

At last they met one of the Hoo-Moo-Loos. He was the funniest little chap they had ever seen in their lives. At first the goblins didn't think he was alive. They thought he was a big ball, rolling along!

That is just what he looked like as he came towards them – but as soon as he came up to them, a head sprang out of the ball, and two arms

49

and two legs jerked out as if they were on springs
– and hey-presto, there was the Hoo-Moo-Loo,
with the roundest, fattest body, and funny little
head, arms and legs!

'Goodness!' said Jinks, in astonishment. 'How
do you do it?'

'Do what?' asked the Hoo-Moo-Loo in a rich,
juicy sort of voice.

'Well, roll along like that?' said Jinks.

'How *do* I?' said the Hoo-Moo-Loo, in surprise.
'Well I might say to you – how *don't* you! It's
much easier to roll than walk.'

'H'm, that depends,' said Jinks. 'Tell me,
is this the land where all the rubbish comes
to?'

'Yes,' said the Hoo-Moo-Loo. 'And do you
know, such a strange piece of rubbish arrived the
other day. It was a little fat, green goblin!'

Jinks and Feefo looked at one another in
delight.

'What's happened to him?' asked Jinks.

'Oh, he was locked up in the Rubbish Cave
because he was rude to King Tick-Tock,' said the
Hoo-Moo-Loo.

'Poor Tuppeny!' said Jinks. 'Where is the
Rubbish Cave?'

'Aha! Wouldn't you like to know!' said the
strange little creature, grinning. He suddenly
shot his head in, jerked his arms and legs into his
ball-like body and became a round, rolling thing

that shot away between Jinks's legs and nearly sent him tumbling to the ground.

'Rude creature!' said Jinks, crossly. They watched the Hoo-Moo-Loo roll away into the darkness.

'Well, it's something to know that Tuppeny is here!' said Feefo, gladly, and he made a noise like six canaries singing loudly.

'What's that, what's that?' suddenly cried dozens of rich, juicy voices, and into the cave rolled about fifty round Hoo-Moo-Loos of all sizes. Some were no bigger than large apples, some were bigger than the goblins themselves. They all shot up heads, and jerked out arms and legs so that in a trice the cave was filled with the funny Hoo-Moo-Loos.

Jinks and Feefo were surrounded by them, and were dragged along to a much larger cave. This was a very strange place, full of ticking, chiming and striking. It was lighted by great lamps set in the walls, and when the two goblins looked round they could see hundreds and hundreds of clocks set on shelves around the cave. At the end of the cave was a throne and on it sat the biggest Hoo-Moo-Loo of all, holding a wrist-watch to his ear to hear it tick.

He wore a crown on his head set with tiny golden watches. It looked very strange.

'He must be mad on clocks!' whispered Jinks to Feefo.

'Silence!' roared the King. 'Who dares to speak when I listen to my new wristwatch ticking?'

Jinks was just going to say something when every clock in the cave began to chime twelve o'clock at once. The King forgot to frown and listened with a pleased smile. But suddenly he sighed and shook his head. He pointed to a large clock on the wall near Feefo and said, 'I suppose you can't tell me how to wind up that clock, goblin?'

Feefo looked at the clock. There was no keyhole anywhere, so it was quite impossible to wind it up. Just as he was about to answer, Jinks gave him a poke in the ribs with his elbow.

'Your Majesty,' said Jinks, breathlessly, 'my friend, Feefo, is marvellous at winding clocks. He can wind this clock up for you, if you like – but you must in return do something for him.'

'Anything, anything!' cried the King, delighted.

'But, Jinks, I can't w –' Feefo began to whisper to Jinks, who gave him another nudge and frowned so fiercely at him that he said no more. Whatever could Jinks be thinking of?

'Well, if you will set free the little green goblin who came here the other day as rubbish, my friend will wind up your clock for you,' said Jinks.

'Will it go if he winds it up?' asked the King.

'That I can't tell you,' said Jinks. 'You can sit by it and wait for it to tick after it has been wound up, if you like. That would be interesting for you.'

'Wind it up, then,' commanded the round, fat King.

'Tell us where the other goblin is, first,' said Jinks.

'He's in the Rubbish Cave, of course,' said the King, impatiently. 'I'll tell one of the Hoo-Moo-Loos to take you there as soon as the clock is wound up. And just you tell that goblin not to be rude to kings next time. He called me a jumping beetle!'

'Oh, but that's just something he says when he's surprised or frightened,' said Feefo.

'Don't argue,' said the King. 'Wind up my clock at once.'

'Go on, Feefo,' said Jinks. But Feefo just stood miserably there, and didn't do anything. 'You silly creature, can't you pretend to take a key out of your pocket and then make a noise like a clock being wound up?' whispered Jinks, fiercely. Feefo's face cleared up at once and he grinned delightedly. Make a noise like a clock being wound up? Ho, that was easy!

He walked over to the clock, and pretended to take a key out of his pocket. It was really only a nail he had there. He pretended to push it into an imaginary keyhole, and then, dear me, bless us all, you should have heard that clock being wound up!

Feefo made a most marvellous noise – a harsh, grating, rusty sort of noise for all the world like a clock being wound up when it has been unwound for hundreds of years. Jinks jumped up and down in delight. How clever Feefo was!

'There you are!' said Feefo, at last, turning to the King, who was listening closely. 'Now if you bring your throne over here and listen for a little while perhaps your old clock will begin to tick. It

may have forgotten how to, so you must tap it
now and again just to encourage it.'

'A thousand thanks!' said the Hoo-Moo-Loo
King, gratefully. 'Hi, Runaround! Take these
goblins to the Rubbish Cave and set the other
goblin there free.'

A small Hoo-Moo-Loo came up. He shot in his
arms and legs and his head too, and rolled away
in front of the two goblins. They followed quickly,
looking round as they left the cave, to see the
King dragging his throne over to his precious
clock!

'You did that well,' whispered Jinks, squeezing
Feefo's hand.

Through many caves and dark passages they
hurried and at last came to one with a large
wooden door, set with huge nails that gleamed
like lamps. A loud voice came from behind the
door, singing a song.

> 'I certainly would never choose
> To make a friend of Hoo-Moo-Loos,
> No, no, no!
> Each one is just a rolling ball,
> I do not like the Hoos at all,
> No, no, NO!'

'That's Tuppeny!' said Jinks, in delight. 'I'd
know his enormous voice anywhere! What a
cheeky song he's singing!'

The Hoo-Moo-Loo with them stood up on his

legs, jerked out his arms and head and unbolted the door. Jinks and Feefo rushed into the Rubbish Cave – and there was fat little Tuppeny, sitting on a pile of rubbish, singing with all his might, while tears poured down his fat cheeks!

'Jinks! Feefo!' he cried, in amazement. 'Is it really you? Oh, how lovely! Oh, you don't know how unhappy I've been! Oh, it was dreadful to tumble into that Witch-bucket and find myself falling into the horrid caves of the Hoo-Moo-Loos!'

'Dear Tuppeny!' said the others, hugging him. 'But you sounded very jolly, singing like that.'

'Oh, that was just to keep my spirits up,' said Tuppeny, wiping his eyes happily. 'Look at this disgusting place they've put me in! They said I was rude to their fat old King, just because I was frightened and said "Jumping Beetles". This is the Rubbish Cave and all the rubbish of the world comes here, I should think!'

There were stacks of papers there, broken pots, bent tins and all kinds of things. As they looked, a heap of green feathers and some odd toadstools came flying down on their heads from the empty air.

'There you are!' said Tuppeny, taking the feathers out of his hat, where some of them had stuck. 'That's the sort of thing that *keeps* happening here!'

'I guess those feathers and toadstools are some of the rubbish that the Windy Wizard has been throwing into his magic bucket,' said Feefo. 'It looks like it!'

'Come on,' said Jinks. 'Don't let's wait here. When the King finds that that silly old clock doesn't go he may come and chase us.'

The three goblins hurried away from the Rubbish Cave, and took a passage that went to the right, away from the King's cave. But they hadn't

gone very far before there came the sound of rolling Hoo-Moo-Loos behind them, and the goblins stopped in alarm.

The Hoo-Moo-Loos jumped to their feet and one of them called to Feefo.

'Goblin! The King wants that key with which you wound up his clock! It has not ticked yet, and he thinks he will wind it up again.'

'I only used a nail,' whispered Feefo to Jinks, in despair. 'Now what are we to do?'

But Jinks was never at a loss. He opened his pedlar's basket at once and felt about in it. Tuppeny could hear the little white mouse squeaking as usual. Jinks found a key and handed it solemnly to the waiting Hoo-Moo-Loos. They took it, made themselves round again and rolled off.

'Quick!' said Jinks. 'They'll certainly be after us again when they find that the key won't wind!'

They hurried on together and at last came to a little cave in which grew a batch of small toadstools, just like the one on which they had come down to the caves.

'Good!' cried Jinks. 'If we sit on these and wish ourselves above ground, we'll be safe.'

Just as they were sitting on the toadstools six Hoo-Moo-Loos came rolling up, shouting, 'What have you done with the keyhole? It isn't there!'

'I wish that we were safely in the open air,' wished Jinks, quickly – and before the Hoo-Moo-Loos could do anything the three toadstools shot up through holes in the cave roof and rose swiftly until they darted out of the ground and came to a stop, sending the three goblins spinning!

'Now run!' cried Jinks, and they ran for their

lives – though they needn't have bothered, for there was nobody after them at all.

Soon they were at Hollyhock Cottage and how pleased Tuppeny was to see it again. He felt as if he had been away for years!'

'Look at all the gold that the Windy Wizard brought us for that Witch-bucket!' said Jinks, shaking out the pieces on the table. 'You shall have most of it, Tuppeny, because you got the bucket!'

'No, let's share alike,' said Tuppeny. 'You rescued me, so it's only fair. We'll all go and buy some new suits and have muffins and crumpets for tea, shall we?'

So out they went, arm-in-arm together, singing for all they were worth!

A Peculiar Adventure in Dreamland

For a week or two the goblins had a lovely time. They spent their money on all sorts of exciting things, especially things to eat. They bought themselves new green suits and new yellow stockings. They spent two gold pieces on a fine armchair and took it in turns to sit in it each night.

Nobody came to order anything from them for two weeks – and then they had their second customer. She came in at the shop door in quite an ordinary way and said 'Good afternoon' very politely.

Jinks got up to see what she wanted. He saw a fairy standing by the counter, dressed in a blue, frilly dress, with great silver wings behind her and the prettiest little face he had ever seen.

'Good afternoon! What can I do for you?' asked Jinks, delighted to see such a pretty visitor.

'Well, you say you can get anything in the world,' said the fairy. 'So I've come to ask you if you'll get me the longest feather out of the Blue

Bird's tail. He lives in Dreamland, you know, and he won't usually let anyone have any of his feathers, not even those that fall out. But I badly want one to stir some magic. The spell *won't* go right!'

'We'd get you *anything!*' said Jinks, smiling at the lovely fairy. 'When do you want it?'

'Oh, as soon as you can get it,' said the fairy. 'My name is Tiptoe and I live next door to you, in Cherry-Tree Cottage. I hope you'll come to tea with me one day.'

'We should be very pleased,' said Jinks. 'Hi, Tuppeny, hi, Feefo, come and be introduced to Fairy Tiptoe. She wants us to do something for her.

Tuppeny and Feefo came running into the shop and stopped in delight when they saw Tiptoe. They shook hands with her, and said yes, of course, they would get whatever she wanted.

'Do you know the best way to go to Dreamland?' asked Tiptoe.

'No, not really,' said Jinks. 'Do you?'

'Yes,' said Tiptoe. 'It is best to go there in your sleep, though some people will tell you that you can fly there by the Dreamland Aeroplane. But that is very expensive and sometimes takes you to Nightmare Land instead, which isn't at all nice.'

'Well, we'll go there in our sleep,' said Jinks. 'We'll go this very evening!'

'Thank you,' said Tiptoe, and ran back to her

own cottage, thinking what nice creatures the three green goblins were.

After the goblins had had tea they got ready to go to Dreamland. They all sat together in the big armchair and Jinks hummed a little magic song to send them to sleep. Presently their eyes closed and Feefo snored very gently. They were asleep!

The armchair they were in began to rock about on its four legs. It rocked to the door and pushed it open. Then it suddenly grew great black wings behind it and rose into the evening sky, flying towards the setting sun. It was strange to see it.

The three goblins slept soundly. The armchair flew on and on and at last came to a land where the sun shone brightly through a misty haze that spread everywhere. This was Dreamland.

The armchair flew gently downwards and landed with a bump in a beautiful garden. The bump woke up the goblins and they sat up and rubbed their eyes. They were most astonished when they found that although they were still sitting in their armchair they were not in their cosy cottage!

'Jumping beetles!' said Tuppeny, of course, looking round. 'Where are we?'

'Well, I suppose it's Dreamland,' said Jinks. 'Come on – we must go and find the Blue Bird if we can.'

'But what about our armchair?' said Feefo. 'We can't leave it here.'

'Well, we must take it with us, then,' said Jinks. 'It's a nuisance, but we simply *can't* leave such a nice chair behind.'

So Jinks and Feefo picked up the big armchair and began to stagger along with it, Tuppeny holding on to one of the legs.

And then, as they went down the path in the garden, a most strange and peculiar thing happened! The armchair suddenly became less heavy and much softer – and before many minutes had gone, Jinks gave a startled shout.

'I say! What's happened! Look at our chair!'

The others looked – but it wasn't a chair any

longer! It was a big, fat baby in a frilly dress and a white bonnet!

The goblins set it down on the grass in astonishment and horror. A baby! What in the world were they to do with a baby? It was so big too – almost as big as they were!

'This is the sort of thing that always happens in Dreamland,' said Jinks, with a groan. 'Things change before you know where you are. What are we going to do?'

'Hoo-hoo-hoo!' wept the baby, very loudly.

'There, there!' said Tuppeny, patting it. 'I say, Jinks, it must be *somebody's* baby, you know. It isn't ours. We can't leave it here, so we'd better try and find out whose child it is.'

'Well, let Tuppeny stay with it whilst we go and find out,' said Feefo. 'We can ask at the big house whose garden we seem to be in. It may even belong there!'

'All right,' said Jinks. 'You can stay here with the baby, Tuppeny. We won't be long.'

Off they went and soon came to a big rambling house which seemed to have no doors at all, no matter where Jinks and Feefo looked.

'Dreamland is a silly place,' said Feefo, impatiently. 'Nothing's ever right.'

Suddenly, round the corner of the house came a fat nurse, wheeling a large pram. She was shaking it gently as she wheeled it and singing a little song. Jinks clutched Feefo and pointed.

'Let's ask her about the baby!'

So they went up to her and bowed.

'If you please, have you lost a baby?' asked Jinks, politely.

'Lost a baby!' said the nurse, in astonishment. She looked into her pram and then gave a loud howl.

'She's gone! The little darling's gone! Oh, where is she, where is she?'

'We know where she is,' said Jinks, eagerly. 'She's down the garden. Bring the pram and you can have her.'

'Did you take her? Oh, you wicked little goblins!' cried the nurse, angrily. 'You wait till I get my precious baby back and I'll soon show you what I'll do to you! Oh, the poor precious thing!'

The goblins ran back down the garden, the nurse following with the pram. But when they reached Tuppeny, they stopped in dismay. There was no baby with him – only a large grey donkey that brayed loudly. It had on the baby's white bonnet and looked very strange.

'Where's the baby?' they asked Tuppeny.

'I don't know,' said Tuppeny, in dismay. 'It suddenly seemed to change into this donkey. I couldn't stop it.'

'Well, *now* what shall we do?' cried Feefo, crossly. 'We've found a nurse who's lost a baby. Look, here she is, and she's jolly angry, too!'

They turned to see her – but even as they

looked the nurse was no longer a nurse but a butcher boy with a large white apron tied round him and the pram was a two-wheeled cart! The donkey backed into the shafts of the cart, the butcher whistled and off they went down the path at a spanking trot, the donkey's bonnet flapping up and down as it went.

'Well, thank goodness that's got rid of the baby!' said Feefo.

'Yes, but we've lost our armchair,' said Tuppeny, sorrowfully.

'Come on,' said Jinks. 'We've got to ask where we can find the Blue Bird.'

They went down the path and out of the gate. Before long they met a man riding on a fat pig and they asked him if he knew where they could find the Blue Bird.

'Yes, it lives with its master, Brownie Long-beard, in the last cottage in the next village,' said the man, and rode off. The pig had changed into a cat whilst he was speaking, but he didn't seem to notice.

The three goblins soon came to the next village. It was a perfectly round place, and each house was set close to its neighbour in a tight circle. So there was neither a last house nor a first one!

Jinks knocked at a door and a little girl opened it.

'Please could you tell me which is the last house in this village?' he asked.

'Yes, it's next to the last but one,' said the little girl, and slammed the door, which immediately disappeared.

'Well, *that's* a lot of help!' said Jinks, in disgust.

'I know!' said Tuppeny, beaming. 'If Feefo can make a sound like bird-seed, perhaps the Blue Bird will look out of one of the windows and we shall see which house the last one is!'

So Feefo made a very strange sound, which made half a hundred brown sparrows at once fly straight on to his head and shoulders! He shook them off, and the three looked carefully round the village. To their enormous surprise they saw a blue bird looking out of *every* window there!

'Oh, well, seeing there are so many blue birds, we might as well choose one,' said Feefo, and he went towards a house. But as he got near to it the blue bird disappeared and seemed to be nothing but a blue curtain waving in the wind. The next blue bird turned out to be a blue vase, and the next one was a piece of blue ribbon tying up a curtain. It was all very puzzling. Dreamland was certainly a peculiar place.

At last, just as they were in despair, they heard the sound of footsteps and saw a brownie coming up to them, with a beautiful blue bird sitting on his shoulder. He had a long grey beard that swept the ground and looked very old and wise.

'Hurrah!' said Jinks, in delight. 'Here's the Blue Bird. Hi, Brownie, would you do something for us?'

'It depends what it is,' said the brownie, stopping. The Blue Bird opened its beak and made a noise like a peacock. Tuppeny nearly jumped out of his skin, for it was a very loud, harsh noise.

'Well, we would very much like a feather out of your bird's tail,' said Feefo. The Blue Bird at once gave a yell and flew straight up into the air. It went to a chimney pot on one of the houses and swooped down it. 'Ho!' thought Tuppeny, 'so that's where it lives.' He looked at the name on the house. It was 'Here-I-Live'. Tuppeny thought that would be nice and easy to remember.

'I might get you a feather if you'll do something for *me*,' said the brownie. 'I want a parcel delivered to Mister Snooze on Up-and-Down Hill. If you take it there safely I'll see what I can do about a feather.'

'Oh, thank you!' said Jinks, delighted. The brownie ran into his house and came out with a large square parcel done up in brown paper and tied with string. He gave it to Jinks.

It was very heavy. Jinks staggered under the weight of it, but Feefo soon gave him a hand. They set off in the direction of Up-and-Down Hill, pointed out to them by Brownie Longbeard.

Halfway there Feefo said he must have a rest, so down they sat, putting the parcel on the ground. But no sooner was it there than it grew six legs and scuttled away from them! Tuppeny jumped up with a shout and caught it.

It grew two hands and gave him a hard smack on the nose! Feefo took it from poor Tuppeny and tucked it under his arm. Then it turned itself into a sort of treacly parcel and flowed away quickly.

'My gracious!' said Feefo, in despair, trying to get hold of it. 'Here, Jinks, you take it!'

Jinks took it and at once the paper fell off, the string became untied and hundreds of papers dropped out and began to fly about in the wind. It was dreadful.

'This is like a bad dream,' said Jinks. He and the others began to pick up the papers as fast as they could, for the wind flew off with them at once. Then, quite suddenly, before they knew how it happened, all the papers flew together, the parcel was done up and tied, and there it was, perfectly good and still, under Jinks's arm!

'Don't let's waste any more time!' said Jinks, and they set off at a run to Mister Snooze's house, which they could see quite clearly on the hill.

The parcel behaved itself till they got there. They knocked on the door but there was no answer. Only a strange noise could be heard. Feefo peeped in at the window and saw Mister Snooze sitting in a chair, fast asleep.

'Let's leave the parcel in at the window and go,' said Feefo. So they pushed the parcel in and turned to go. But that wretched parcel began to make a noise like a horse neighing and woke up Mister Snooze at once. He rushed to the window and called out, 'Hi, you! That's my horse got out of the field again. Put him back, will you?'

'No, it isn't!' said Jinks. 'It's the parcel we brought you from Brownie Longbeard making that noise!'

A loud neigh sounded in his ear and he turned round – and to his enormous astonishment he saw a little horse just by him! How strange!

'You might take him to Longbeard's!' called Mister Snooze. 'He wants to borrow him to go to market.'

Jinks caught hold of the halter round the horse's neck and led him off. The others came with him, glad that the wretched parcel was at last delivered. The horse lagged behind a little after a bit, and Jinks pulled him. 'Come on, there, come on!'

He turned to see why the horse was so long in coming – and bless us all, there wasn't a horse on

71

the end of the rope at all! There was a large
hippopotamus!

'Jumping beetles!' shrieked Tuppeny, and took
to his heels at once.

Jinks stared at the hippo in dismay, but it
seemed quite harmless, if a little slow. It came
quietly lumbering on, blinking at Jinks out of its
little eyes.

'I don't know what Longbeard will say if he sees
us bringing him a hippo instead of a horse,' said
Jinks. But Tuppeny and Feefo were too far ahead
to hear him. They didn't like hippos quite so
close!

However, Jinks needn't have worried – because
by the time the hippo reached the village it
wasn't a hippo any more, but a nice fat pig, wear-
ing, for some strange reason, galoshes on its four
feet.

'Where does the brownie live?' asked Jinks as
they came into the village.

'He lives at "Here-I-Live",' said Tuppeny,
pleased that he had noticed the name.

The first house they looked at was called 'Here-
I-Live', so Jinks went up the path and knocked
at the front door. A cross-looking woman opened
it and asked them what they wanted.

'Will you tell Longbeard we have come back?'
said Jinks. The woman made a face at him and
answered crossly.

'What are you talking about? Brownie Longbeard doesn't live here! He lives in the last house.'

'Well, Tuppeny, you are *silly*!' said Jinks, annoyed, going back down the path. 'You might have noticed the name of Longbeard's house properly. He doesn't live there!'

They went to the next house – and dear me, *that* was called 'Here-I-Live' too! And so was the next one – and the next one – and all of them. It was too silly for words.

There was nothing for it but to knock at every house, and find out if Longbeard lived there. They went all round the village, and, of course, it was the very last house they knocked at that was the right one.

'Well, everyone said Longbeard lived in the last house, and they were right,' said Jinks, gloomily. 'This is the silliest place ever I knew!'

Longbeard asked them in at once. He gave them some chocolate cakes which tasted of ginger and some cocoa to drink which tasted of lemonade. The Blue Bird sat on his shoulder all the time and blinked at the goblins. In its tail was a very long feather indeed and Jinks longed to have it.

Longbeard didn't seem to mind at all having a pig instead of a horse, to ride to market, so that was all right. When they had finished eating Jinks reminded him politely that he had promised them a feather out of the Blue Bird's tail.

'Well, you can get one if you like,' said the brownie, grinning. Jinks was delighted. He at once made a grab at the Blue Bird who gave a loud squawk and flew round the room. The three goblins chased it, each trying to get the long blue feather. But that bird was very artful. It always just managed to get out of the way. It hid behind things, it flew up to the ceiling, it ran under the table.

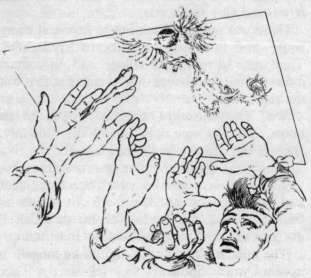

But at last Jinks caught it. Yes, he actually did! He got it by the tail and carefully pulled at the longest feather there so as not to hurt the lovely bird.

And even as he pulled, a peculiar and most annoying thing happened. The bird changed into a blue monkey and goodness, gracious me, Jinks pulled its tail out! There it was in his hands, a blue, hairy tail, not a bit feathery, not a bit like a bird's! The monkey darted up to the top of the curtains and sat there, tailless, scolding Jinks hard in a loud, chattering voice.

'Look here!' said Jinks, crossly, to the grinning brownie. 'This won't do, you know! Change that monkey back into a bird again at once and let me have a feather. You promised!'

The brownie only laughed loudly, and Jinks became angry. He rushed at Longbeard – and then, in a trice, everything broke up and disappeared! It was very strange. The walls of the cottage fell in with a bang, the roof flew off, and the whole village, with the brownie and the Blue Bird too, disappeared like a flash of lightning.

Only the three goblins were left. They stood amazed, Jinks holding the monkey's tail in his hand. Nothing was left of the village at all – except one small armchair just behind them.

The goblins sat down in it, too astonished to speak a word. Suddenly they felt sleepy. Their heads fell forward and Feefo began to snore gently.

And, as soon as they were asleep, that little armchair rose up into the air and grew wings! It flew away to Heyho Village, came gently to the ground, pushed open the door of Hollyhock Cottage and went inside.

After a short while the three goblins woke up. They looked all round and were most astonished to find that they were home again – and even more surprising still, in their own armchair! Wasn't that amazing?

'It must all have been a dream!' said Tuppeny, yawning.

'No, it wasn't,' said Jinks, flapping the monkey tail at him. 'Look here!'

Just then, there was a knock on the door and Fairy Tiptoe came in.

'I heard you talking, so I knew you were back,' she said, excitedly. 'Did you manage to get me that feather?'

'No,' said Jinks, sadly, shaking his head. He held out the monkey tail. 'This is all we got.'

'But that *is* just the very feather I want!' said Tiptoe, and she took it gladly from Jinks – and as she took it, it changed into a long, waving blue feather! It was very extraordinary.

'You darlings!' cried Tiptoe, and gave them each a kiss. They *were* pleased. 'Now you shall come to tea with me and taste my new chocolate cake. It's very good. And I will give you each ten pieces of gold for being so clever.

'We don't want the gold,' said Jinks. 'We just want your friendship, Tiptoe. We'd *love* to come to tea with you!'

A Peculiar Adventure in Dreamland

That new chocolate cake *was* lovely! Jinks had two pieces, Tiptoe had one, Feefo had three and Tuppeny had four – so there wasn't much left, as you can imagine!

The Castle of the Booming Giant

The very next day there came another customer to Hollyhock Cottage. This was a small red dwarf who drove up in a bright green motorcar, which stopped outside the cottage and hooted very loudly indeed.

Jinks and the others peeped out of the window. When they saw the red dwarf they didn't like the look of him at all. He was a most disagreeable creature, dressed very beautifully in red satin trimmed with real gold buttons. In his hat was a jewelled feather and on his long nose were spectacles set with diamonds that flashed brilliantly every time he moved his head.

He hooted loudly again.

'I suppose he wants us to rush out and bow to him,' said Jinks, in disgust. 'Well, he can want!'

'Hoot-hoot-hoot!' went the car, and all the neighbours put their heads out of their windows to see what the noise was about.

Jinks stuck his head out too.

'What are you hooting for?' he shouted. 'Is there something in your way?'

'I want to speak to you,' said the dwarf.

'Well, *I* don't want to speak to *you*!' said Jinks, and slammed the window.

'You'll be sorry!' shouted the dwarf, angrily. 'I'm the richest dwarf in the world, and I can pay you well for anything you sell me.'

'Well, let me sell you some good manners, then!' said Jinks, opening his window and grinning at the angry dwarf. 'They don't cost much and you could do with them!'

The dwarf glared at Jinks. Then he opened the door of his car, got out and marched up the path.

Tuppeny was frightened. 'Jumping beetles, Jinks, here he comes! You oughtn't to have spoken to him like that.'

The dwarf knocked at the door. Jinks opened it and the dwarf came in.

'You're a bold one, to talk to *me* like that!' he said to Jinks. 'No one has ever spoken to me like that before. You must be very brave.'

'Did you want to buy some good manners, then?' asked Jinks, smiling wickedly.

'No,' said the dwarf, shortly. 'Don't be rude any more. I don't like it. I should have gone away when you spoke to me so cheekily, but because I thought it was brave of you to say what you really thought, I hoped you might be the kind of fellow who could get me what I wanted.'

'And what is that?' asked Jinks, Tuppeny and Feefo, all together.

'I want to buy the pair of red shoes that the Booming Giant has,' said the red dwarf. 'I believe he will sell them if you offer him three of my largest diamonds to wear in his cap.'

'The Booming Giant!' said Jinks, astonished. 'But my goodness me, we'd never come back if we went to see *him*!'

'Oh, I'll give you a Get-away spell,' said the red dwarf. 'He will certainly want to keep you prisoners, but he won't be able to if you use the Get-away spell.'

'All right,' said Jinks. 'We'll get the red shoes for you – though why you want them I can't imagine, when you can buy any amount at the cobbler's!'

'Never you mind what I want them for,' said the red dwarf. He put his hand in his pocket and took out a small leather wallet. He undid it and the three goblins gasped – for inside lay three of the largest and most beautiful diamonds they had ever seen! They winked and blinked as if they were alive.

'Jumping beetles!' said Tuppeny, in awe.

Then the dwarf took out a little blue box and showed the goblins a tiny pinch of purple powder inside it.

'This is the Get-away spell,' he said. 'All you have to do when you want to escape from the

Booming Giant is to scatter this powder in front of you. Then you will get away perfectly easily.'

Jinks took the wallet of diamonds and the blue box and put them safely into his basket.

'We'll go tomorrow to the Booming Giant,' he promised. 'We'll let you know when we've got the red shoes for you.'

The dwarf said goodbye, ran down to his car and drove away. The three goblins rubbed their hands and did a little dance. 'We shall soon be very, very rich!' they sang. 'We shall soon be very, very rich!'

They went to say goodbye to Fairy Tiptoe next

81

door, and she was sorry to hear they were going away.

'It won't be for long,' said Tuppeny, hopefully.

'How do we go, Jinks?' asked Feefo, waggling his ears, feeling excited to think there was another adventure coming.

'The Booming Giant lives in the Thunder-Clouds,' said Jinks, who was busy unfolding a map. 'Look, there they are. We've got to go to the Sugar Mountain, whose tip sticks into the clouds. The Booming Giant lives in a castle at the top.'

Next morning they set off together, and went to catch the little train that ran through the country-side to the Sugar Mountain. They took their tickets from the big grey rabbit who sat in the ticket-office and waited for the train.

It came puffing in at last, not much bigger than a toy train, with open trucks to sit in, instead of proper carriages. It was full of gnomes and brownies, all chattering hard, and it was difficult to find places.

Nobody would move up and make room for the three goblins. But Feefo soon made them! He made a noise like a growling tiger, and you should have seen how those gnomes and brownies got out of his way! There was plenty of room at once!

Jinks and Tuppeny giggled. 'Where's the tiger?' called Jinks to Feefo. 'Is he going to run along beside our truck?'

Goodness, how those gnomes and brownies shivered and shook.

'That will teach them manners!' whispered Tuppeny to Jinks.

The train went on for a long way and all the gnomes and brownies got out at a station called 'Fair Station.' There was always a fair there, and the goblins could hear the roundabouts playing in the distance.

Tuppeny wanted to leave the train and go and look at the fair, but Jinks said no, certainly not! They were on business, and it would be silly to go to a fair with three large diamonds. Somebody would be sure to steal them.

So on they went in the little, puffing train. It went into a dark tunnel and then out again. It went over a long, high bridge that ran across a very wide green river on which floated tiny blue-sailed boats. It looked very pretty, and Tuppeny was so interested in leaning out and watching the ships that he very nearly tumbled right down into the river below.

Jinks caught him just in time. He grabbed him by the leg and pulled him into the truck.

'Ooh! Don't!' said Tuppeny, very red in the face, rubbing his leg. 'You clumsy thing, Jinks, hurting my leg like that!'

'Well, really!' said Jinks, crossly. 'I just saved your life, Tuppeny, and that's all the thanks I get! You might have been in the river by now.'

'Well, next time you save my life you needn't grab my leg quite so hard,' grumbled Tuppeny, sulkily.

The train went on and on, past Twisty Station and Tumble-down Station and many more. At last the three goblins gave a shout and pointed to a curious hill in the distance. It shone like white sugar, and reached up so high that its top was quite hidden in some very black, thundery-looking clouds.

'There's the Sugar Mountain!' cried Jinks. 'Hurrah! We're nearly there.'

The train puffed right up to the foot of the curious, sugary mountain and then stopped at a little station there called Sugar Station. The three goblins got out of their truck and the train went on round the mountain.

'The thing is – how do we get up?' said Feefo, rubbing his long nose.

'There aren't any steps,' said Tuppeny.

'The sugar slips dreadfully when you tread on it,' said Jinks. 'It's like loose white sand. We'll never be able to get up this hill!'

Just at that moment a most surprising thing came round the corner of the hill. It was a camel! There was no one with it, which made it all the more astonishing. It came straight up to the three goblins and knelt down in front of them.

'What does it want?' said Tuppeny, getting behind the others in a fright.

'It's come to take us up the Sugar Mountain!' cried Jinks, delighted. 'Camels can walk easily on sand, so this one won't find it at all difficult to climb up on sugar! Good camel! Fine camel!'

The camel made rather a nasty, cross sort of snort that Tuppeny didn't like at all. Jinks hastily got on its hump and Feefo and Tuppeny climbed on to its neck. The camel stood up and began to climb the Sugar Mountain. The goblins had to hold on very tightly, for the camel slanted steeply as it climbed and it swayed from side to side in a very alarming manner.

'Get up, there! Get up, there!' cried Jinks, encouragingly, but the camel only made a few more nasty noises. It really was a very bad-tempered sort of beast.

The mountain was very high. There seemed to be no paths of any sort, no grass, no trees, no bushes – only just gleaming white sugar. The camel went up and up, grunting and gurgling, and the goblins clung on for dear life.

'We're coming to the Thunder-Clouds!' cried Jinks, at last. The others looked up. Sure enough, not very far above them were the heavy-looking purple clouds they had seen from the train.

'I can see the giant's castle in the clouds!' said Tuppeny, nearly falling off the camel as he looked upwards. 'Ooh! Jumping beetles, it *is* a monster castle!'

So it was! It was bigger than anything the goblins had ever imagined, and its towers and turrets rose gleaming towards the sun, which peeped here and there between the moving clouds.

'Gurgle-grr-gurgle,' said the camel, in its cross voice and knelt down on a cloud, which, although it seemed very flimsy indeed to look at, seemed to be hard enough to walk on, though it felt rather spongy to the foot.

'It's like walking on a terribly thick carpet,' said Tuppeny. 'I do hope I shan't suddenly walk in a hole and fall right down to the earth below.'

'You'd better take my hand in case you do,' said Feefo. 'You're a dreadful goblin for falling out of things.'

Hand in hand they walked over the soft thunderclouds towards the towering castle. A long flight of steps led up to a gleaming black door, set with yellow stones of some kind.

'What are we going to do?' whispered Tuppeny to Jinks. 'Are you just going straight in to ask for the shoes, or what?'

'Yes, I think so,' said Jinks, boldly. 'I've got those three lovely diamonds to offer the giant. I expect he'll be pleased to give us the shoes in exchange.'

So they knocked at the great door, and it opened slowly before them. A booming voice, like the wind at sea, came through the door.

'BRING THE WASHING IN, AND PUT IT DOWN, MRS DOWELL.'

Jinks and the other two stepped inside the door, and blinked in amazement, for there, before them, was the very biggest giant they had ever seen in their lives. He was as tall as the tallest tree, and his eyes were as large as cartwheels and so blue that they seemed like ponds in his face.

'If you please, we're not the washing,' said Jinks.

'SPEAK MORE LOUDLY,' said the giant, not looking up from the book he was reading.

'WE'RE NOT THE WASHING!' shouted Jinks, Tuppeny and Feefo, together. That made the giant look up and he seemed most surprised to see the three goblins.

'Then what are you?' he boomed.

'We're three goblins who have come to buy something from you,' said Jinks, boldly. 'We want a pair of red shoes you have, and we have brought three large diamonds to pay for them.'

'Let me see them,' said the giant, greedily. Jinks undid the wallet and the three stones glittered brilliantly before the astonished giant.

The giant calmly put down his enormous hand and took the wallet from Jinks.

'Thank you!' he said, with a thunderous laugh. 'I'll keep them. As for the shoes, they are not for sale.'

'But you can't keep the diamonds if you don't give us the shoes!' cried Jinks, horrified.

'Can't I?' grinned the giant, showing two rows of white teeth as large as piano keys. 'I can! And what's more, I'm going to keep you too! Ho, ho, that's a good joke!'

Tuppeny began to weep. He was scared out of his life. Feefo went red with rage and Jinks for once in a way really didn't know *what* to do or say!

The giant picked them all up and popped them into a big wastepaper basket, so high and tall that the goblins couldn't possibly get out of it.

'You stay there for a bit,' he said. 'I'll sell you to the Wandering Wizard when he comes to see me tonight. He'll be glad to have you.'

The three goblins crouched together in the bottom of the basket.

'It's all your fault for being so silly as to walk in boldly like that,' wept Tuppeny to Jinks. 'We ought to have found out what sort of a giant he was first.'

'I'm awfully hungry,' said Feefo, sighing. 'I wish we had something to eat.'

Jinks opened his basket. He really did feel ashamed of himself to think he had landed his friends into such terrible trouble. To Feefo's great delight there were packets of chocolate and three apples in the basket. The mouse was there too, just beginning to nibble one of the apples. Jinks took that one for himself, smacked the mouse and divided up the rest of the food between the others. They all ate in silence, wondering whatever they could do to escape.

They tried to get out of the basket. It was no good at all, and the giant heard them scrabbling about and roared to them to keep quiet.

'I'm trying to work out a spell!' he boomed. 'How can I work when you make such a noise, like a lot of fidgety mice. Be quiet or I'll put you in the dustbin.'

After that the goblins didn't dare to move! The afternoon came and the giant got himself tea. Darkness fell and the giant lit a great lamp that shone almost as brightly as the sun itself! He bent over his spell, frowning.

Suddenly Feefo, who had been thinking very hard, made a noise like six cats fighting each

other. It made Jinks and Tuppeny almost jump
out of their lives, and they glared angrily at Feefo,
who calmly went on making the extraordinary
noise.

'Drat those cats!' shouted the giant, crossly. He
went to the window, threw it open and shouted
'BE QUIET, WILL YOU?' to the cats he thought
were quarrelling outside his window. For a while
Feefo made no noise – then he began again, and
this time it seemed as if there must be fifty
cats, by the hissing and snarling, wailing and
groaning!

The giant jumped up in a rage and took a big
jug of water to the window. He threw the water
where he thought the cats were and Feefo stopped
snarling at once. The giant went back to his work.

Then once more Feefo began, this time like a
hundred cats, and the giant went nearly mad with
rage. He threw his boots at the cats, he threw a
kettle and he threw a chair. Then he flung open
his china cupboard and was going to throw out all
his cups and saucers when Feefo poked his head
nearly out of the basket, standing on Jinks's
shoulders.

'Please, sir, I can stop those cats for you, and
send them away.'

'You!' said the giant, scornfully. 'Why, they are
giant cats and would gobble you up like a mouse,
goblin.'

'Well, let me try,' said Feefo.

'Very well,' said the giant, grinning, 'but don't blame me if you get eaten, that's all! And mind you come back once you've scared them away!'

'Oh, yes!' said Feefo. He whispered something very quickly in Jinks's ear and then the giant hauled him out of the basket.

'Before I go, do tell me where you keep the red shoes,' begged Feefo. 'I know it's no good asking you for them, but I *would* like to know where they are kept.'

91

'Well, much good may it do you!' said the giant. 'I keep them in my pocket!'

Feefo said nothing more, but went to the door, which the giant opened for him, and slipped out into the darkness. He began to shout as if he were scolding a great many cats, and very soon there came a sound as if dozens of cats were scampering away. The giant was pleased. He went to the door and looked out for Feefo – but he was nowhere to be seen.

'Come back!' shouted the giant. But Feefo didn't come back. He was safely at the bottom of the Sugar Mountain, having rolled all the way down in a great hurry!

'Let me go and find him!' cried Tuppeny to the giant. 'Give me a lantern and let me go. Feefo can't see in the dark and maybe he has lost his way going after the cats. I will bring him safely back.'

The giant lighted a small lantern and gave it to Tuppeny. It was almost as big as he was, but he managed to carry it. He ran out of the door, calling Feefo. But as soon as he was out, he threw the lantern down and rolled himself over and over in the sugar, right down to the very bottom of the hill, just as Feefo had done.

He bumped into Feefo, who caught him and hugged him. 'What about Jinks?' asked Tuppeny.

'Oh, he's going to get the red shoes when the giant is asleep, and then use the Get-away spell,' said Feefo, grinning in the darkness. 'We'll wait here for him!'

'I do hope he won't be long!' sighed Tuppeny, who was very tired of this adventure. 'I want to be safely at home in dear little Hollyhock Cottage!'

Jinks and the
Surprising Shoes

Jinks sat at the bottom of the wastepaper basket
alone, glad that Tuppeny and Feefo had managed
to escape. The giant was very angry when he
found that the others did not come back. He
roared and stamped till the castle rocked quite
dangerously on the clouds.

Then he looked into the basket and shook his
fist at Jinks, who pretended to be frightened. He
wasn't really, because he had the Get-away spell
safely in his basket, and knew he could escape at
any time – but he meant to get those magic red
shoes first!

'I'm going to have a nap until my friend, the
Wandering Wizard, comes,' roared the giant.
'And don't you think you can play any tricks
on me as your friends have done, because you
can't!'

'Oh, no, I shouldn't dream of it,' answered
Jinks, politely. The giant went to a big armchair
and lay back on the cushions. He closed his eyes
and in a moment or two there came the sound of

snoring. It sounded like fifty motorcars starting up their engines, and almost deafened Jinks.

He grinned to himself, and then opened his basket. The little white mouse was there, and when Jinks spoke to it, it pricked up its tiny ears and listened hard.

'I want you to nibble a hole in this big wastepaper basket I'm in,' said Jinks. 'Can you do that, little Whiskers?'

The mouse squeaked and jumped out of Jinks's tray at once. It ran to the side of the big waste-paper basket and began to nibble hard. Soon there was quite a big hole in it, and Jinks was able to make it bigger by tearing it open with his hands. The mouse went on nibbling and nibbling. It had very sharp teeth and was pleased to be able to help Jinks.

'Get back on to the tray,' whispered Jinks to the mouse, when he saw that he could just squeeze through the hole. The mouse ran up Jinks's leg and hopped on to the tray. Jinks shut it up and made it into a basket again. Then, taking a peep through the hole first, he squeezed through and found himself standing on the floor of the giant's hall.

The giant was still snoring loudly, and the castle shook to the sound. Jinks stole quietly up to the sleeping giant and climbed silently up the chair-leg. He squeezed himself on to a small piece of the armchair seat and tried to see into the

giant's pockets. They were as big as caves to
Jinks!

He could see nothing inside at all. It was too
dark. So there was nothing for it but to creep right
into the pocket and see if the red shoes were there!

Jinks was brave. He began to worm himself into
the pocket, hoping and hoping that it was the
right one. It was! He felt a pair of shoes there, not
very big, almost his size. He carefully pulled at
them and took them into his hands. Then he
began to crawl out of the giant's pocket.

And just at that very moment there came a
thundering knock at the castle door which woke
up the giant!

It was the Wandering Wizard! He came stalk-
ing in, crying, 'Good evening, good evening! And
how is my friend the Booming Giant tonight?'

The giant jumped up and shook hands. The
Wandering Wizard was a strange fellow with a
long beard that he kept tied in a neat knot at his
waist. He seemed quite a jolly chap, and Jinks,
peeping out of the giant's pocket, wondered if he
were very powerful. It would be dreadful if he was
powerful enough to stop the Get-away spell from
working!

'I've got a surprise for you!' said the Booming
Giant to the wizard. 'I had three little green
goblins here today, and I thought I'd give them
to you for servants. But two got away, and I've
only one left.'

'Dear dear, stars and moon, couldn't you manage to keep the lot of them?' said the wizard. 'You are really rather a stupid fellow, Booming, though I like you well enough. Well, where's the third goblin?'

'In that wastepaper basket,' said Booming.

The wizard went over to it.

'There's nothing there but a large hole in the side,' he said, surprised. 'Are you playing a joke on me?'

'Of course not!' said the giant, astonished. He looked into the basket too, and when he saw that Jinks had escaped he went as red as a tomato with rage.

'So he's gone too,' he roared. 'Well, I've got their diamonds, anway. Look, Wizard – three beauties to put into my cap. They came to get my magic red shoes. Aha, little do they know the magic that is in those shoes. Only those who wear the shoes know that!'

'Where are the shoes?' asked the wizard. The giant put his hand into his pocket – and brought out Jinks! Jinks had carefully packed the shoes into his basket for safety and had also quickly taken out the Get-away spell which was in its little box.

'Why, here's the third goblin!' cried the giant. 'In my pocket! After those shoes, I'll be bound! Oh, the rascal, oh, the wretch, he's taken them, he's taken them!'

Jinks slid out of the giant's hand and jumped to

the ground. He ran about the kitchen, laughing,
for he thought he would tease the giant.

'Ho ho ho!' he grinned. 'I've got the shoes, dear
giant! Catch me if you can! Ho ho!'

Then began such a chase! The wizard ran after
Jinks, and so did the lumbering giant! Jinks
darted under sofas and tables, he ran into corners,
he hid under rugs. The wizard and the giant were
quite out of breath trying to catch the slippery
little goblin.

And at last the giant *did* catch him! He made a
dart at him and his fingers closed over the

wriggling goblin – but at that very moment Jinks blew the purple powder out of the box and cried, 'Get me away spell!' – and hey presto a big wind came, swept him out of the giant's hand, through the open window and down to the bottom of the Sugar Mountain!

Tuppeny and Feefo had fallen fast asleep there, waiting for him. They woke with a jump as he rolled into them, and when they struck a match and found it really was Jinks, they were too delighted for words.

Jinks told them all that had happened and showed them the red shoes safely packed in his basket. The white mouse was curled up in one of them and looked very comfortable indeed. Jinks stroked him and called him a little hero for helping him to escape from the wastepaper basket.

'Let's make a cosy hole in this sugar and go to sleep again,' said Tuppeny, who was yawning widely. So they dug a big hole with their hands, crept into it, curled up together like kittens and fell sound asleep.

They awoke when the sun was high in the sky. The camel woke them by grunting and bubbling in their ear. He butted them with his nose and then knelt down to take them on his back.

Tuppeny was just about to get on him, when Jinks pulled him back.

'Don't be so silly!' he said. 'That camel would

only take you back to the castle! He won't take us home.'

'Oh, won't he?' said Tuppeny, who was often rather stupid. 'Well, I won't ride him then. Shoo, camel, shoo!'

But the camel wouldn't shoo. It made some very nasty noises and showed them its teeth – so the goblins decided they had better move away.

'We'll catch the first train back to our village,' said Jinks, firmly. 'Oh, do go away, camel. We don't WANT you!'

They soon left the camel behind and made their way to Sugar Station. The train came in and they got in. It was quite empty this time, so they had it to themselves. They passed all the stations they had passed before, and at last came to Fair Station. There was the fair beginning again! They could hear the music of the roundabouts and see the swings going high in the air.

'Oh, Jinks, dear Jinks, do let's go to the fair!' begged Tuppeny. 'We've done our work and got the red shoes, and it would be nice to have some play now. Besides, I'm very hungry and we could get breakfast at the fair. I know they have fried sausages and new bread because I can smell them from here.'

'Come on, then!' said Jinks. They all tumbled out of the train and were soon eating plates of steaming sausages and munching rolls of new bread. They drank hot coffee and felt very much better. Then they went on the roundabouts and on the swings and had a fine time.

Soon Jinks got excited and thought he would show off a bit. So he put his hat on his feet, turned himself upside down, and began to walk on his hands, just as he had done when Feefo and Tuppeny had first seen him.

But the fair-ground was muddy and Jinks's hands got very dirty. He remembered the red shoes in his basket and took them out. He slipped them on his hands and then began to walk upside down again, waggling his feet about with his hat on them, and dancing the red shoes about on his hands. Tuppeny and Feefo stood and giggled at him and the fair-folk shouted in delight.

Then, as Feefo and Tuppeny stood watching him Jinks began to walk out of the fair-ground! He walked right out of the gate!

'Hi, Jinks, where are you going?' shouted Tuppeny. 'Come back! You're going the wrong way!'

Jinks shouted something back but the others couldn't hear him. They ran after him and caught him up. Jinks was now walking on his hands very fast indeed and they could hardly keep up with him.

'Jinks, Jinks, where are you going, you silly?' cried Feefo, in fright.

'I can't stop!' cried Jinks, in a scared voice. 'It's

these magic shoes I've put on my hands, Feefo. They are taking me away. Can you get them off?'

Feefo tried his best to snatch at the shoes, but they went faster and faster as he tried to grab at them.

'Where are they taking you to?' shouted Tuppeny.

'Back to the Booming Giant's, I'm afraid,' yelled Jinks. 'I ought to have remembered that they are magic.'

At that the red shoes began to run so fast that Tuppeny and Feefo were left far, far behind. Soon poor Jinks was nothing but a small speck in the distance, hurrying back to the Sugar Mountain.

Tuppeny burst into tears.

'Now what are we to do?' he wailed. 'After getting the magic shoes and all, and escaping so nicely, there's poor Jinks gone back to the giant, who is sure to be very, *very* angry with him!'

Feefo was very pale. This was dreadful. Jinks had no Get-away spell this time.

'We'd better go back home,' he said, 'and see if the dwarf will give us another Get-away spell.'

So they jumped into the first train home and sent a message to the Red Dwarf. But when he heard what had happened, he laughed mockingly and shook his head.

'No,' he said. 'Get-away spells are most expensive. I'm not wasting any more on you. Let Jinks escape by himself this time. He shouldn't have been so stupid as to wear the red shoes. He knew they were magic. They always take anyone back to Sugar Mountain Castle.'

The two goblins were very unhappy. They sat in their big armchair together and even Feefo couldn't help the tears dripping down his cheeks.

There came a knock at the door, and Fairy Tiptoe came in. She was most astonished to see them so upset.

'Whatever's the matter?' she asked. 'And where's dear Jinks?'

They told her – and she listened with wide eyes.

'How dreadful!' she said. 'However can we rescue him?'

'We can't,' sobbed Tuppeny. 'Nobody can.'

'Oh, there must be a way,' said Tiptoe, thinking hard. 'I wonder if my grandmother would lend me her big, invisible cloak. Whoever wears it cannot be seen, you know. If we went to Sugar Mountain we might be able to smuggle Jinks away under the cloak.'

'Oh, let's try!' said Feefo, at once. So Tiptoe ran off to her grandmother's cottage and, as she had been very good and kind to the old lady, she was quite willing to lend her the magic cloak, if she promised not to tear it.

'Here it is!' said Tiptoe, coming in at the door. 'Now watch!'

She wrapped the shining blue cloak around her and at once she and the cloak disappeared entirely. It was marvellous! Both the goblins had to try it, of course, and laughed to see each other disappear like smoke!

They ate a good dinner and set off in the afternoon to go back to the Sugar Mountain, making plans on the way. The disagreeable camel was there, and they all clambered on to his back, though Tiptoe was just a bit afraid of him.

When they got to the Thunder-Clouds Tiptoe scooped some of the clouds out and made a little hiding-place for them so that the giant should not see them if he looked out of the window.

'Now this is my plan,' she said. 'First I will put on my magic cloak so that the giant won't see me, and I'll go and tell Jinks we're here and what to do. Then I'll come back to you and we'll see what to do next.'

The little fairy pulled the blue cloak round her and at once disappeared. She flew to the castle and entered in at the open window. Jinks was inside, tied to a table leg with a thick rope so that he couldn't move. The giant was peeling potatoes and talking loudly and scornfully to Jinks.

'Jinks, Jinks!' whispered Tiptoe, flying down beside him. He was startled because he could see nobody. He looked round, half scared.

'It's I, Tiptoe,' whispered the fairy, and she told

him how she and the others had come to rescue him.

'Can you think of a good plan?' she whispered. Jinks thought hard – and then he whispered into Tiptoe's ear. She nodded her head, gave him a little kiss on his right ear and flew out of the window again, pulling the giant's hair on the way, which astonished him very much indeed, for, of course, he could see nobody at all!

Tiptoe told Feefo and Tuppeny the plan and they agreed. They hid in the little cloud-hole until it was dark and then they crept out. Tuppeny and Feefo stood just outside the open window, and then, at a sign from Tiptoe, they began to make a noise!

Feefo made a noise like a roaring dragon in a temper! You should have heard him! It was perfectly marvellous, really! Even Tuppeny felt a bit frightened, though he knew it was only Feefo.

Tuppeny's part was easy. He had to shout at the top of his very big voice, crying, 'Come here, Dragon! Come here, I say!'

You see, they were pretending that a dragon had escaped and had come to the castle, and that Tuppeny was trying to catch him! Then Tiptoe did her part. She left the magic cloak with Feefo, who had it ready for Jinks when he should come out. She flew in at the window and blinked in the light of the bright lamp inside.

The giant had jumped to his feet in fright when he had heard the roaring of what he thought was a fierce dragon. Jinks was pretending to be frightened too, but he wasn't really, for he knew it was only Feefo.

'Oh, please, oh, please!' panted Tiptoe to the giant, pretending to be very much frightened. 'Will you come out and catch the dragon? He's escaped and we can't get him.'

'Of course I won't come and catch the dragon!' said the giant, hastily. 'I don't do silly things like that. Chase it down the mountain at once.'

'But he wants to come and see you,' said Tiptoe.

'See ME!' said the giant, in a terrible fright. 'Whatever for?'

'He says he's never tasted giant,' said Tiptoe.

'Ow-oo-ah!' yelled the giant, wondering wherever he could hide. But he was so big that he couldn't possibly hide himself anywhere.

'Has he ever tasted goblin?' suddenly asked the giant, hopefully.

'No, never,' said Tiptoe.

'Well, ask him if he'd like to taste a nice little goblin I've got here,' said the giant.

So Tiptoe called this out of the window and the dragon roared pleasantly that he would like very much to see the goblin. So the giant undid the rope that tied Jinks to the table and he ran out of the door. As soon as he reached Feefo that goblin threw the magic cloak around him, and around himself and Tuppeny too, and stopped roaring. Tiptoe flew out and joined them. She crept under the big cloak, and they all lay still to see what would happen.

The giant was puzzled. Where was everyone? What had happened to the dragon? Where was that little fairy? And suddenly he saw that he had been tricked! It was no dragon! It was only somebody roaring like one!

With a roar even louder than Feefo's the angry giant rushed out of his castle with a bright

107

lantern. But no matter where he looked he could *not* see the goblins and the fairy. They were invisible, hidden under the magic cloak.

The giant ran shouting down the hill, trying to find them – and immediately Jinks ran back into the castle, opened a cupboard and took out the red shoes, which the giant had put there when he had taken them away from Jinks.

He popped them into his basket and ran to join the others.

'We'd better go down the other side of the Sugar Mountain,' said Tiptoe. 'Then we shan't run into the giant!'

It was much easier to climb down the other side. They were soon at the bottom. Then they saw the two red lights of the little train that ran around the mountain and they stopped it by pulling up the signal. They climbed on board and off they went, all very tired, very happy and very hungry.

They got home just as the sun was rising in the east. They were so sleepy that they could hardly eat the eggs that Tiptoe boiled for them or drink the cocoa she made.

'Oh, Tiptoe, we're *so* grateful to you!' said Jinks, half asleep. 'We'll never forget your help! Whatever the dwarf gives us for getting the red shoes, you shall share!'

And what do you think he gave them? Why, his green motorcar! So Tiptoe had to share that, and went for many a ride with the three goblins. Feefo usually drove because he was the most careful of the three, and when the horn went wrong, he could make a lovely honking noise. It was really lovely to hear him!